WHY DO ANIMALS SMELL Like THAT?

Reese Everett

Rourke
Educational Media

rourkeeducationalmedia.com

Scan for Related Titles
and Teacher Resources

Teaching Focus:
Consonant Blends: Look in the book to find words that begin with a consonant blend such as *st, sm,* or *pr.*

Before Reading:

Building Academic Vocabulary and Background Knowledge
Before reading a book, it is important to set the stage for your child or student by using pre-reading strategies. This will help them develop their vocabulary, increase their reading comprehension, and make connections across the curriculum.
1. Read the title and look at the cover. *Let's make predictions about what this book will be about.*
2. Take a picture walk by talking about the pictures/photographs in the book. Implant the vocabulary as you take the picture walk. Be sure to talk about the text features such as headings, Table of Contents, glossary, bolded words, captions, charts/diagrams, and Index.
3. Have students read the first page of text with you then have students read the remaining text.
4. Strategy Talk – use to assist students while reading.
    - Get your mouth ready
    - Look at the picture
    - Think…does it make sense
    - Think…does it look right
    - Think…does it sound right
    - Chunk it – by looking for a part you know
5. Read it again.
6. After reading the book complete the activities below.

Content Area Vocabulary
Use glossary words in a sentence.

boundaries
carcass
musky
predators
prey
territory

After Reading:

Comprehension and Extension Activity
After reading the book, work on the following questions with your child or students in order to check their level of reading comprehension and content mastery.
1. *What do possums do to protect themselves from predators?* (Summarize)
2. *What do vultures do when they feel threatened?* (Asking questions)
3. *What does a hoatzin smell like to ward off predators?* (Text to self connection)
4. *What do some animals use their scents for?* (Inferring)

Extension Activity
Think about all the animals you read about in the book and how they use smell to protect themselves or to find each other. Now, do some research. Using the Internet, find other animals and see what defense mechanisms they use to stay safe. Record your findings in a journal or notebook and share them with your classmates!

Table of Contents

Stinky, but Safe

You smell something yucky. Do you want to eat it? Or do you want to get far away from it?

Some animals can make themselves stinky for protection.

Predators hunt for fresh **prey.** Possums pretend they are dead to avoid a predator's attack.

A possum playing dead produces a strong odor. It smells like a rotting **carcass**.

The possum's act wouldn't scare away a vulture. These birds look for dead animals to eat.

Vultures also have a smelly defense system. When they are threatened, they vomit on their attacker. The smell of the rotting carcasses they eat scares away predators.

Hoatzins are stinky birds, too. They smell like cow poop! Their odor also repels predators.

Hoatzins eat mostly leaves. They digest their food through fermentation, like cows. This makes the birds smell like cow manure.

Skunks can't outrun most predators. They spray them with a stinky fluid instead. The foul odor can be smelled from a mile (1.6 kilometers) away.

The lesser anteater is even smellier when it feels threatened. Its spray is seven times stronger than a skunk's. Not many predators want to eat something that smells so rotten!

White-tailed deer produce a stinky, waxy substance from glands in their hooves when they sense danger. A deer will stomp its hooves to leave the scent as a warning to other deer in the area.

Smells Like Home

Some animals use scents to mark **territory**. Wolverines produce a strong **musky** odor.

When a wolverine claims an area, it leaves this scent everywhere to let others know to stay out of its range.

A musk ox uses its smelly urine to mark the **boundaries** of its territory.

The musky urine often gets all over the ox, too. This makes the animal stink!

Humans can't smell ants. But ants can! An ant's body odor indicates the nest it belongs to and its job within the nest.

If an ant goes into the wrong nest, its scent will alert other ants that it is an intruder. It will be attacked.

Elephant shrews live in pairs. The pair is rarely together, though. They keep track of each other by leaving scent markings within their shared territory.

Love Is in the Air

Some animals use odors to attract mates. During mating season, male and female alligators release a strong scent from glands under their jaws.

Female moths produce a scent that male moths can smell from miles away.

Bola spiders release an odor that mimics the scent of a female moth. This brings a tasty male moth flying straight toward the hungry spider.

Humans cannot smell all of the odors animals produce. That may be lucky for us!

Photo Glossary

boundaries (BOUN-dur-ees): Lines or markers that separate one area from another. Animals use scents to mark the boundaries of their territories.

carcass (KAR-kuhs): The dead body of an animal. A possum releases a scent that smells like a rotting carcass.

musky (muhsk-ee): Having a smell that suggests musk, a chemical produced by some animals.

predators (PRED-uh-turs): Animals that live by hunting other animals for food.

prey (pray): An animal that is hunted by another animal for food.

territory (TER-i-tor-ee): An area of land claimed by a particular animal or group of animals.

Index

Websites to Visit

kids.nationalgeographic.com

www.sciencekids.co.nz

www.animalfactguide.com

Meet The Author!
www.meetREMauthors.com

About the Author

Reese Everett is a writer, mom, and fan of animal videos from Tampa, Florida. When she's not writing, you can find her watching her kids play sports or reading by the pool.

Library of Congress PCN Data

Why Do Animals Smell Like That?/ Reese Everett
(Why Do Animals...)
ISBN 978-1-68191-727-6 (hard cover)
ISBN 978-1-68191-828-0 (soft cover)
ISBN 978-1-68191-922-5 (e-Book)
Library of Congress Control Number: 2016932651

Rourke Educational Media
Printed in the United States of America, North Mankato, Minnesota

Also Available as:

www.rourkeeducationalmedia.com

Edited by: Keli Sipperley
Cover design, interior design and art direction: Nicola Stratford
www.nicolastratford.com

PHOTO CREDITS: Cover © Debbie Steinhausser; page 4 © Kamira; page 6-7 © Sari ONeal; page 8 © Veselin Gramatikov, page 9 © Mattias Lindberg; page 10 © Kent Ellington, page 11 © Debbie Steinhausser; page 12 © © Lukas Blazek, page 13 © FotoRequest; page 14-15 © Erik Mandre; page 16 © Dennis W. Donohue, page 17 © by pap; page 18 © pavel dudek, page 19 © Orhan Cam; page 20 © AleksandarMilutinovic, page 21 © Johnwoodkim All photos from Shutterstock.com except page 12 Dreamstime.com

Animals don't use soap, but that's not why they smell funny sometimes. An animal uses body odors to help it survive in the wild. Their scents are also used to communicate with other animals. Find out how animals use different scents in *Why Do Animals Smell Like That?*

Alignment

This title supports NGSS standards for Biological Evolution: Unity and Diversity. Readers will learn about the diversity of life in various habitats and how animals are equipped to function in their environments.

Books In This Series Include:

Why Do Animals
Eat That?

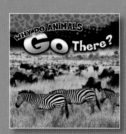
Why Do Animals
Go There?

Why Do Animals
Hide?

Why Do Animals
Live There?

Why Do Animals
Look Like That?

Why Do Animals
Sleep There?

Why Do Animals
Smell Like That?

Why Do Animals
Sound Like That?

ISBN: 978-1-68191-828-0

90000

9 781681 918280

Rourke
Educational Media
rourkeeducationalmedia.com